Bea & Bee

by
Sylva Fae

Dedication

For my bushcraft buddies:
Alexandre da Rocha, Gray Durgan,
Naomi Tayler, Carl Dobson
and Leslie Swain.

Also by Sylva Fae

Rainbow Monsters Series
Rainbow Monsters
Winner of Chanticleer Little Peeps Award - Best in Category
Mindful Monsters

Children's Christmas Collection
With authors Kate Robinson,
Paul Ian Cross and Suzanne Downes

No Place Like Home

Yoga Fox

That Pesky Pixie
www.getbedtimestories.com/library/that-pesky-pixie

An Itchy Situation
A Stinky Start!
A Dastardly Plan
A Feast for a Fairy Queen
Three Pesky Pixies and a Monstrous
Mouse

Beatrice was her shouting name.

"BEATRICE ROSE! Don't flick your peas!"

"BEATRICE ROSE! Get back in bed!"

"BEATRICE ROSE! Don't pick your nose!"

But the rest of the time she was just Bea. She was a happy Bea.

Bea lived in a little cottage just outside the village. Her friend Poppy lived next door with her puppy, Pip. Bea longed to have a pet, but Mummy said:

"Our garden is just too small for a dog, Bea."

Bea's garden wasn't really a proper garden. It was more of a back yard with a small patch of soil along the edge, where Bea grew flowers.

Flowers made Bea happy.

In winter, snowdrops brightened
the drab yard.

In spring, Bea's yard started to fill
with colourful flowers.

In summer, the dandelions and
daisies grew wild.

And by autumn, the sunflowers
had grown as tall as Bea.

Bea loved her flower patch even though it was too small for a dog. She loved to water it and sing to the flowers.

One day, as Bea was humming, she heard a buzzy sound. Bea stopped humming and looked around. The buzzing stopped too. Bea started humming again and the buzzy sound joined in.

Sitting on a sunflower was a
fuzzy buzzy bee.

"Hello little bee, I'm Bea too.
I shall call you Little Bee,
just like me."

Little Bee crawled onto Bea's
finger and waved his front leg.

Bea and Little Bee sat in the
flower patch together. Bea
hummed and Little Bee buzzed.

"Hey Little Bee, you can hum
just like me."

Soon Mummy called Bea in for tea.

"Bye bye Little Bee," called Bea as she skipped to the door.

Little Bee tried to follow her but he went...

ziggedy zaggedy

wibbly wobbly plop!

Bea ran to pick him up.

"Be careful Bea! It might sting you."

"It's OK Mummy, Little Bee is my pet," she said stroking Little Bee's fuzzy back.

"You can't keep a bee as a pet!"

"But Mummy, you said our garden is too small for a dog, but it's the perfect size for a bee."

Mummy couldn't argue with that.

Bea put Little Bee in Mummy's
flower pot.

"Hey Little Bee, you can have
tea just like me."

After tea Bea ran out to play with Little Bee.

Little Bee flew to greet her.

ziggedy zaggedy

wibbly wobbly plop!

Bea joined in.

She ran ziggedy zaggedy wibbly wobbly and plopped onto the grass next to Little Bee.

"Hey Little Bee you can fly just like me!"

Mummy peeped her head out of
the door.

"I think your little bee has a
poorly wing. He can't fly
straight."

Bea had a close
look. Mummy was
right. Little Bee's
wing was torn.

"Poor Little Bee. I'll look after
you until you're better."

"Snack time!" called Mummy, bringing out a tray of drinks - a juice for Bea and a plate of sugary water for Little Bee.

Little Bee drank thirstily.

"Hey Little Bee, you can drink just like me."

That night Mummy put Bea to bed, but after she'd kissed her good night, Bea ran to the window.

"Night night, Little Bee," she called.

Little Bee flew…

ziggedy zaggedy

wibbly wobbly plop!

He landed on the windowsill.

Bea grabbed a pillow from the
dolls house and made Little Bee a
cosy bed.

"Hey Little Bee, you can sleep
just like me."

The next day Bea was excited. Mummy was taking her out to lunch. Of course Little Bee came too, perched in the basket of Bea's bicycle.

As Bea and Mummy found a table
in the sunshine, Little Bee buzzed
over to the florist next door.

ziggedy zaggedy

wibbly wobbly plop!

Little Bee
landed on a
pot of lavender.

"Hey Little Bee, you can have lunch just like me."

Mummy had grown to like Little Bee.

"If Little Bee is going to be your pet, we need to do some shopping," she said.

Bea, Mummy and Little Bee
went to the garden centre.

They watched while Little Bee
pointed out his favourite
flowers.

Little Bee helped Bea push the trolley to the checkout.

"Hey Little Bee, you can do shopping just like me."

After tea, Bea played with Poppy and Pip while Mummy planted all the flowers.

When Bea returned home, she found her drab yard had been transformed into a colourful garden.

Little Bee flew to greet her.

ziggedy zaggedy

wibbly wobbly plop!

He landed on Bea's nose.

Bea heard lots of loud buzzy
sounds and looked around. Bees
buzzed and butterflies fluttered
from flower to flower.

"Hey Little Bee, now you have
friends just like me."

The End

Note from the author

If you find an exhausted or injured bee the best thing you can do is place them in a sheltered part of the garden, near to bee-friendly plants.

Bee-friendly trees and flowers
Spring
Pussy willow, apple or crab apple, crocus, lungwort, marjoram, cowslip, comfrey

Summer
Lavender, hawthorn, monarda 'bee balm', phacelia, chives, wood forget-me-not

Autumn
Abelia, honeysuckle, sedum, perennial wallflower, sage, yarrow

Winter
Mahonia, ivy, winter aconite, snowdrop, marjoram, lesser celandine

If this is not possible, you can help revive a tired bee with a little drop of sugar water.

Sugar water

Mix half a teaspoon of white refined sugar with half a teaspoon of warm water.

- Do not feed bees brown sugar or honey.
- Do not leave out bowls of sugar water for bees. This can actually do more harm as the bees will drink the sugar water instead of flower nectar – it's the equivalent of feeding them junk food. Sugar water is great as a quick energy boost for a tired bee but it is not a replacement food source.

About the Author

Sylva Fae is a married mum of three from Lancashire, England. She grew up in a rambling old farmhouse with a loveable but slightly dysfunctional family and an adopted bunch of equally dysfunctional animals.

As a college lecturer and verifier, she has spent twenty years teaching literacy to adults with learning difficulties and disabilities.

Sylva and her husband own a wood where they run survival courses and woodland craft days. Adventures in the woods inspired her to write stories to entertain her three girls. Her debut children's book Rainbow Monsters won the Chanticleer Best in Category award.

Sylva Fae writes a blog:
sylvafae.co.uk

Come say hello on Facebook.
www.facebook.com/SylvaFae

Or Twitter
https://twitter.com/sylvafae

Printed in Great Britain
by Amazon